HOW PEOPLE ARE POISONING THEMSELVES - AND WHAT TO DO ABOUT IT.

PROCESSED
FOOD

BY

MIGNONNE GUNASEKARA

All rights reserved.
Printed in Malta.

A catalogue record for this book is available from the British Library.

ISBN: 978-1-83927-453-4

Written by:
Mignonne Gunasekara

Edited by:
William Anthony

Designed by:
Danielle Rippengill

©2021
BookLife Publishing Ltd.
King's Lynn
Norfolk PE30 4LS

All facts, statistics, web addresses and URLs in this book were verified as valid and accurate at time of writing. No responsibility for any changes to external websites or references can be accepted by either the author or publisher.

Image Credits

All images are courtesy of Shutterstock.com, unless otherwise specified. With thanks to Getty Images, Thinkstock Photo and iStockphoto. Cover: wow.subtropica, Rayyy, sokolovski, Milan M, Olga Miltsova, udra11. 4 – Jack Frog. 5 – Tomsickova Tatyana. 6 – Ahanov Michael. 7 – Vladimir Nenezic. 8 – luchschenF. 9 – Shestakoff. 10 – Niloo. 11 – Feng Yu. 12 – vystekimages. 13 – Stokkete. 14 – HandmadePictures. 15 – Ekaterina_Minaeva, Ron Dale. 16 – Africa Studio, Motortion Films. 17 – didesign021. 18 – junpinzon, Stephen McCluskey. 19 – Midhat. 20 – wavebreakmedia. 21 – EKramar. 22 – Elena Sherengovskaya, Hafiez Razali. 23 – Arayabandit, D. Pimborough, Moving Moment, MWPHOTOS55.

CONTENTS

PAGE 4   Too Much of a Good Thing
PAGE 6   What Is Processed Food?
PAGE 8   Additives
PAGE 10 Preservatives
PAGE 12 Badditives
PAGE 14 Ingredients to Watch out For
PAGE 18 Unhealthy Cooking
PAGE 20 A Healthy Diet
PAGE 22 Food Swaps
PAGE 24 Glossary and Index

Words that look like this can be found in the glossary on page 24.

Too Much of a Good Thing

Cooking is a great way to spend time with your loved ones.

We all need food to live. It gives us the strength to grow, run and learn. It can also be tasty and fun!

However, there are certain types of foods that can be bad for us, especially if we eat them a lot. What happens to our bodies when we eat these foods?

Some **ingredients** and ways of cooking can make food unhealthier.

What Is PROCESSED FOOD?

Processed food is any food that has been changed from the way it is found in nature. Any food that isn't processed is raw.

Freezing, canning and drying are all ways of processing food.

Processing food can be very helpful. It can help keep food fresh so we waste less of it.

Not all processed foods are bad. We just need to watch out for the unhealthy ingredients and ways of cooking that processing foods can bring.

ADDITIVES

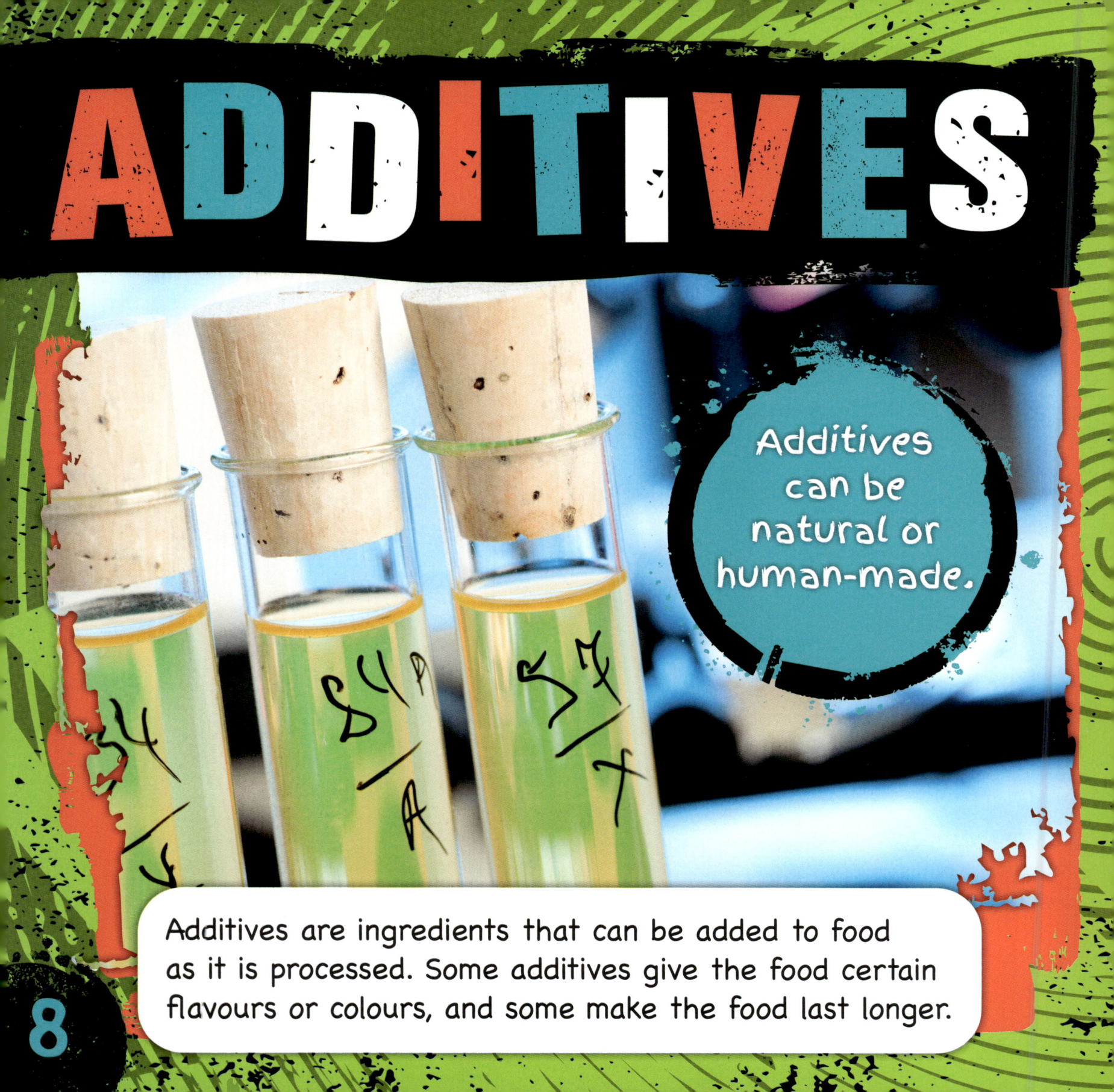

Additives can be natural or human-made.

Additives are ingredients that can be added to food as it is processed. Some additives give the food certain flavours or colours, and some make the food last longer.

Some additives hold food together, almost like glue. These kinds of additives might be used in some types of ice cream. Other additives can make food tastier.

PRESERVATIVES

Additives that make food last longer are called preservatives. Preservatives allow food to be moved all over the world without going bad.

Have you ever noticed the expiry dates on packaging?

An expiry date can also be called a 'use by' date or a 'best before' date.

This date tells us when the food is no longer safe to eat. With the help of preservatives, the expiry date can be much later than normal.

BADDITIVES

Some people can be sensitive to additives.

This means they might have a bad reaction to them. They may get an upset stomach or hives if they eat food with certain additives in them.

People who are sensitive to some additives need to carefully read food packaging. This helps them to stay away from foods that use those additives.

In most countries, packaging must say which additives are in the food.

INGREDIENTS to WATCH OUT For

Salt

Some ingredients can lead to health problems if we eat too much of them. A little bit of salt, sugar or fat is fine, but how do we check if we are eating too much of them?

Many countries around the world use colours on the packaging to show the amount of salt, sugar and fat in the food. This is a quick, easy way to check how healthy the food is.

Sugar and salt are used to make food taste better. You shouldn't worry about eating a little of these things. However, eating too much of them can be bad for you.

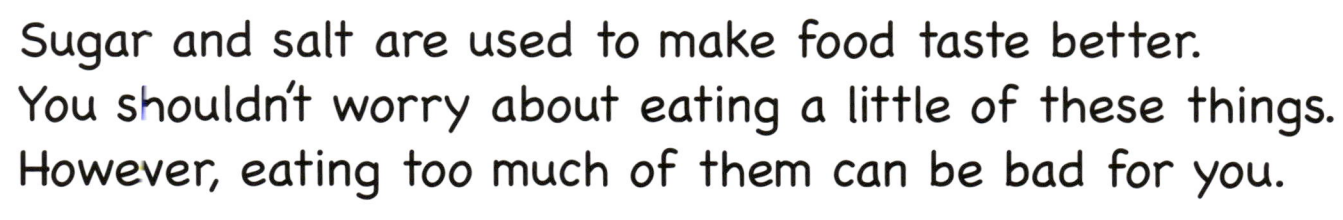

Salt and sugar are often found in foods such as pizza or chocolate.

Children aged four to six should have fewer than 19 grams of sugar and 3 grams of salt a day.

Eating too much sugar could lead to **tooth decay** or health problems such as **diabetes**. Too much salt could cause **heart disease** later in life.

UNHEALTHY COOKING

Some ways of cooking can make foods unhealthier. Here are some of those ways.

Frying in oil

Boiling vegetables too much is not good. They lose a lot of their nutrients in the water.

Deep-fat frying is one of the unhealthiest ways of cooking food. Chips, doughnuts and fried chicken are often deep fried.

Deep fat frying

A HEALTHY Diet

Meals should have a **starchy** food, such as potatoes, pasta, rice or bread.

A healthy diet might include some beans, eggs, meat or fish.

For a healthy diet, you must eat lots of different types of foods. Make sure you eat five **portions** of fruit and vegetables each day.

Eating fresh food is very healthy for us. Cooking it in a healthy way is also important. For example, steaming vegetables is very healthy.

Vegetables in a steamer

FOOD SWAPS

Here are some foods you can swap to have a healthier diet.

Have low-fat milk instead of whole-fat milk.

If you want something sweet and sugary, have some fruit instead.

Sausages and pizza have lots of bad fat. Avocado, fish and seeds are full of good fat.

Have a plain yoghurt with banana instead of a sugary yoghurt.

For a snack, try some malt loaf instead of chocolate.

Eat a **wholegrain** cereal instead of a sugary cereal.

GLOSSARY

diabetes	a disease in which the body has trouble controlling blood sugar levels, which can lead to damage to organs
heart disease	damage or illness that affects the heart
hives	a red rash on the skin that itches a lot
ingredients	foods that are mixed or cooked together to make a meal
nature	everything in the world around us that was not made by humans
nutrients	natural substances that plants and animals need to grow and stay healthy
portions	the right amounts of food you should eat in one sitting
raw	uncooked or unchanged
reaction	in sickness, getting feelings of illness from something such as nuts
starchy	full of lots of starch, which is a tasteless, white part of food from plants
tooth decay	when teeth become rotten
wholegrain	contains the whole of the grain seed and all of the nutrients – nothing being removed

INDEX

additives 8–10, 12–13
beans 20
boiling 18
dairy 9, 22–23
fish 20, 23
freezing 6
fruit 20, 22–23
frying 18–19
meat 19–20, 23
packaging 11, 13, 15
salt 14–17
sugar 14–17, 22–23
vegetables 18, 20–21, 23